HICCUP

The Viking who was Seasick

to my father

Gather round,
said the ancient crab,
and hear the tale of

HICCUP

The Viking who was Seasick

by Cressida Cowell

Hodder
Children's
Books

A division of Hodder Headline Limited

Long ago, in a fierce and frosty land, there lived a small and lonely Viking, and his name was Hiccup.

Vikings were enormous roaring burglars with bristling moustaches who sailed all over the world and took whatever they wanted.
Hiccup was tiny and thoughtful and polite.
The other Viking children wouldn't let him join in their rough Viking games.
Hiccup was frightened of spiders. He was frightened of thunder. He was frightened of sudden loud noises.

BANG!

But most of all he was frightened of going to sea for
the very first time … next Tuesday.
Hiccup wasn't sure he was a Viking at all.

'Only girlies

Hiccup's father was **Stoick the Vast.**

Wherever Stoick walked the ground trembled, flowers wilted and bunnies fainted. He hadn't brushed his beard in thirty years.

brush their beards!'

boomed Stoick the Vast.

'Girlies don't have beards,' Hiccup pointed out,
but no one listened to him.

And when Hiccup told his father he was frightened of
going to sea, Stoick laughed his enormous Viking laugh
until the salty tears ran down to his enormous hairy feet.

'You can't be frightened, little Hiccup.

Vikings don't get frightened.'

And he sang the Viking Song:

I have blacked the 1,000 eyes

OF 1,000 angry GALES

Watch me knock the cockles off

The biggest blue-est WHALES

I have given walrus nightmares

Who thought that they were STRONG

He patted Hiccup on the head and went off to do
three hundred press-ups before breakfast.
'Oo-er,' thought Hiccup. 'It all sounds very dangerous.'

So Hiccup went to see the oldest Viking of all, Old Wrinkly
himself, whose barnacled beard fell down to his toes.
'Your Saltiness,' he whispered (for Hiccup had beautiful
manners), 'do Vikings ever get frightened?'

'Little grandson,' wheezed Old Wrinkly, and his breath was like being kissed by mackerel, 'I've been wondering about the answer to that question myself. The sea is full of trials and terrors. But it is also full of marvels and miracles. Go to sea and you can tell me if Vikings ever get frightened.'

So, at a quarter to nine on a breezy Tuesday . . .

. . . Hiccup went to sea for the very first time.

At half past nine, Hiccup
was wishing he hadn't
eaten those two small-ish
haddock for breakfast.

At a quarter
to ten he was feeling
very peculiar indeed.

And, at half past ten,
he wished he was dead.

'I feel seasick,' he
said to his father.
'Vikings don't get seasick,'
said Stoick the Vast.

But this one was, all over Stoick's feet.

Hiccup got sicker and sicker . . .

. . . and the storm got wilder and wilder.

Stoick the Vast sang the Viking Song at the storm.
But the storm took no notice.
A great wave came up and soaked him.

One mighty wave picked up that whole Viking ship as if it were a matchstick and threw it fifty miles to the south. And one mighty blast from the gale picked up that whole Viking ship as if it were a piece of seaweed and threw it fifty miles to the west.

And a terrible black wind went shrieking all over the lonely ocean and turned that Viking ship upside-down and inside-out and went shivering down every single Viking's spine.

'We're lost,' said Stoick the Not-So-Vast-After-All. And a funny thing happened. His face began to turn a greenish hue, and he thought of the thirty-seven large-ish haddock he had had for breakfast . . . and his stomach began to heave.

And then all the Vikings turned a pretty green colour and all their stomachs heaved and with an almighty rush they ran to the side . . .

'Well, well,' said Hiccup. 'It appears
that Vikings DO get seasick.'
And immediately he began to feel better.
'This direction!' shouted Hiccup.

But the Vikings were too busy
being seasick to steer the boat.
So Hiccup began to take charge.
And a funny thing happened.
The more he steered, the better he felt.

As he headed for home that stormy wind filled the sails and the
boat skimmed over the ocean at one thousand miles an hour.
Out of the depths of the sea came shoals of flying fish, and
leaping dolphins, and strange whales with horns like unicorns.

There were eels that lit up like lightbulbs, and nameless things with enormous eyes that no one had ever seen before - all following Hiccup the Viking as he steered that ship at tremendous speed towards home.

'Nice breezy day,' hummed Hiccup as he
steered into the harbour.

'So tell me,' said Old Wrinkly - and
his old whelk eyes might have
been twinkling - 'do Vikings
ever get frightened?'

'Sometimes they do,' said Stoick the Vast.

'But they get over it,' said Hiccup the Viking.
'That's what makes them so BRAVE.'

Vikings ~~Never~~ Sometimes get Seasick

The End

Hiccup
The Viking who was Seasick
by Cressida Cowell

British Library Cataloguing in Publication Data
A catalogue record of this book is available from the British Library
ISBN 0 340 75721 3 (HB)
ISBN 0 340 75722 1 (PB)

First hardback edition published 2000
First paperback edition publidshed 2001
10 9 8 7 6 5 4 3 2 1

Published by Hodder Children's Books,
a division of Hodder Headline Limited,
338 Euston Road, London NW1 3BH

Printed in Hong Kong